Snow What Fun!

WHEN SNOWMEN COME TO LIFE ON CHRISTMAS EVE

D1400653

SNOW WHAT FUN!
When Snowmen Come to Life on Christmas Eve

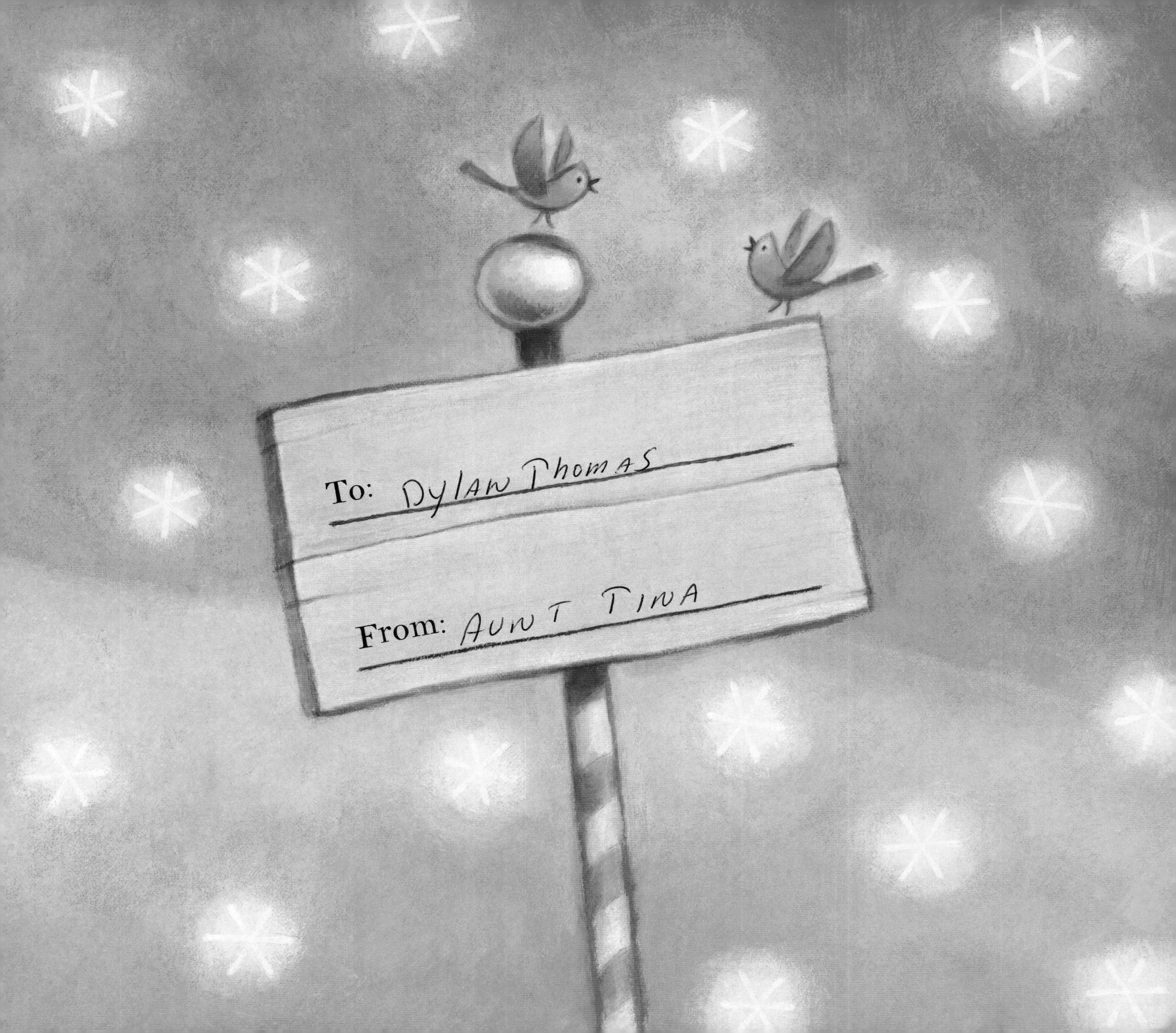
To: Dylan Thomas
From: Aunt Tina

'Twas the night before Christmas, and all through the land,

the snowfolks were stirring according to plan.

They sprang into life in a fluffy white flurry
and fled from their yards in a great big fat hurry
into the streets, where they shouted with glee,
"Hooray, now it's time for the Snow Jubilee!"

They clumped and they clustered, said "Howdy" and "Hi," then smooshed into snow clouds and swooshed through the sky...

...past forests and rivers and over a knoll
to a most secret place that's just south of North Pole.

From all over the planet,

they started arriving

and greeted each other with hugs

and high-fiving.

'Twas their once-a-year snow night,

their big rendezvous,

but first...

they had something important to do.

"Look," someone shouted. "Up there—it's his sleigh! We've got to guide Santa—no time to delay!"

So quickly they lined up (their form was **perfection**)

and waved **Santa's sleigh** in a southbound direction.

Then they took out their banjos,
their flutes, and their drums.

They sang silly songs,
and they hummed happy hums.

They waltzed and they polka'd.
They jived and they jumped.

They pranced and they chicken-danced.
Man, were they pumped!

They staged a big contest with fabulous games. They awarded the winners and called out their names...

Now Slushy,

now Freezy,

now Twirly,

now Twiggles.

On Jingle,

on Bingle,

on Wheezy,

on Wiggles.

They snapped on their snowshoes, their skis, and their skates and **barreled** about at incredible rates.

And when they were tired, they flopped to the ground, enjoying their bird friends who flocked all around, feeding them seeds they had brought in big sacks. (It felt really good just to rest and relax.)

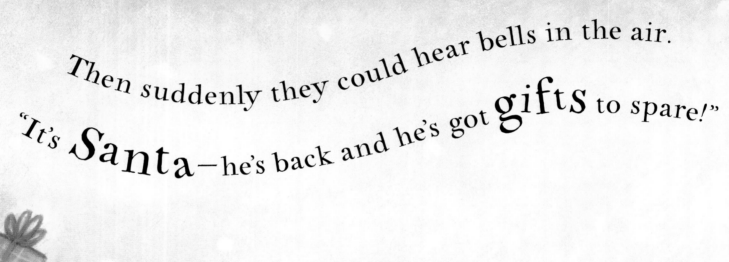

Then suddenly they could hear bells in the air.
'It's Santa—he's back and he's got gifts to spare!"

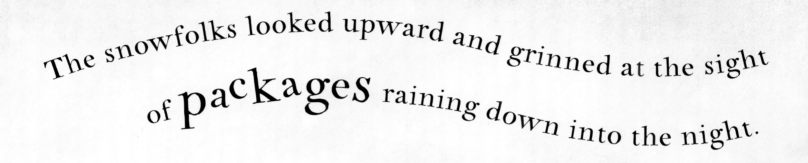

The snowfolks looked upward and grinned at the sight
of **packages** raining down into the night.

"Wow,

what a fabulous Snow Jubilee—

but the night's almost over,

so we'd better flee!

We've helped out old Santa

and had some fun, too.

Mission accomplished—

it's time to skiddoo!"

Softly they swooped up in balls of white fluff
and lumpily, bumpily flew fast enough...

...to arrive in their places before the sun rose

and return (every one!) to their regular pose.

Now maybe you're thinking it's hard to believe

that snowpeople come to life each Christmas Eve.

But look out your window first thing Christmas Day...

and see if your snowman looks quite the same way!